SECOND STRIKE

THE THRILLING SEQUEL TO

FIRESTORM

By Jessica Schluff

To my sister who inspired me to follow my dreams by following hers

Copyright 2017

all rights reserved

PART ONE – CURTAIN RISING

Chapter 1

Police Captain Montgomery Snowden watched an undercover operation playing out on his desktop computer in real time.

Under other circumstances, Snowden would be thrilled to see Donna Sparks, one of his finest detectives, taking part in such an important federal operation, but this time he was nervous. Snowden could see that the agent that his detective was responsible for supporting was distracted and Snowden was concerned that Agent Firestone's lack of focus could get his detective killed.

Snowden was right to worry. Special Agent Anthony Firestone's mind was stuck on loop. A thousand images of past events from his career were surging through him, reviving thousands of emotions.

Eleven years ago, Agent Firestone had been dispatched overseas as the FBI's part of an international and interagency taskforce. The taskforce was made up of three CIA agents, an NCIS agent, a SEAL team, and Firestone and was designed to eradicate a vicious and lucrative human trafficking organization that called itself the Scarlet Orchid.

The Scarlet Orchid focussed mostly on prostitution and mail-order brides, but it also used its profits to fund thousands of other criminal activities; including supporting mob families, orchestrating arms deals, arranging contract killings, supporting drug cartels, and financing terrorism. Naturally, collapsing the organisation was vital to national security and the best way to collapse it was to put its mastermind behind bars.

Back then, Amilio Scarleto, the crazed madman behind the Scarlet Orchid and the taskforce's target, escaped after wounding CIA Agent Leah Fong.

Firestone, Fong, and the rest of the team were dispatched to a clinic in Iraq first. On the surface, the clinic simply treated the sick, but the team uncovered that it was funded by Scarleto so they knew that no one was being cured there; only paying men and enforcers were allowed in.

When they finally cleared out the clinic, at the cost of two SEAL's lives, Scarleto escaped and managed to smuggle his trafficked women out of the Middle East with him.

What was left of the taskforce eventually followed Scarleto and his group of thirty-four kidnapped women into Africa; where, through layers of chatter, they believed that Scarleto's girls were being held at a girl's school in Zambia. When they arrived in Zambia however, they found a burned out crater where the school should have been.

Apparently, a local gang that was against women's education hosted a bonfire, during which, the school was burned at the stake. All of the students and staff were killed in the fire and, supposedly, Scarleto's girls were counted among the victims, but the local government refused to let the taskforce examine the bodies so they were never certain of whether Scarleto's girls were actually among the dead.

Firestone refused to believe Scarleto would let so much equity burn. He insisted that the girls were still at the site where the school belonged because his research told him that the school had a storm bunker below it that was built to withstand attacks like the one the school had suffered specifically.

Firestone believed Scarleto chose that school because of that bunker because it was secure and secret; it was an ideal hiding place for hostages, but only Leah stuck with him to search it.

Before they could search the bunker however, Scarleto dashed out from the jungle shadowing the school and without additional support, Firestone and Fong were forced to ignore the hidden bunker in favor of apprehending their target.

Firestone was conflicted about whether he should search the bunker or run out to assist Leah, so he was left behind in the jungle when he finally decided to follow her. The distance between them ensured that he was unable to assist Leah until Scarleto was long gone, but as he called and gathered the rest of the taskforce to their location from his clearing in the jungle, he heard Scarleto and Leah in the heat of conflict.

He remembered hearing Leah identify herself as a federal agent and demand that Scarleto stop. Her shouts were immediately followed by the grunts and thuds that help Firestone envision a vicious martial arts battle, but because of the geography of the jungle, he couldn't find them; all he could do was listen.

Eventually, a shot was fired, which Firestone later learned was Scarleto shooting Leah, and then Firestone heard Scarleto say something about being disappointed that he would never traffic Leah because she was doomed to die slowly. Scarleto then started his plane and the draft from the climbing plane helped Firestone find his way out of the jungle because the wind gust bent the underbrush and finally gave Firestone a direction.

Firestone was too late to stop Scarleto, but he administered life-saving first-aid to Leah.

The rest of their team eventually found them thanks to Firestone's call and aided them the rest of the way, but because their efforts to arrest Scarleto catastrophically failed; Leah and Firestone were forcibly evacuated.

That mission cost Leah her career at the CIA, but she joined Firestone at the FBI and while Leah jovially declared it their first mission as partners, Firestone always blamed himself for Leah's career being damaged, her being injured, and the fact that Scarleto's girls were never found to his satisfactory.

Once they were state-side, it was up to the military to try to locate Scarleto and because the military believed the government's story that Scarleto's missing girls had been killed at the school fire, they refused to consider Firestone's bunker theory; instead, they focussed on the jungle that Scarleto had come from to hunt for him.

The military believed that Scarleto had turned one of the logging encampments located deep in the jungle into another base after the school burned and they focussed on searching the logging camps for *possible* leads where Scarleto *might* go instead of finding where the girls were or where Scarleto's plane went, so Firestone made it his life's mission to bring Scarleto to justice and hopefully resolve what happened to the thirty-four women Scarleto had trafficked.

Firestone got an opportunity to fulfill his mission against Scarleto approximately five months ago when a group that was working for Scarleto disguised a simple contract killing as terrorism by staging a bombing on the Carlton Tower.

The Carlton Tower was once the epicenter of both business and pleasure in the city. In addition to being home to more than a hundred rental suites, doctor's offices, medical labs, server rooms, and banking offices; the Carlton Tower also held the world's largest shopping mall at its base and it hosted the world's largest casino on its top floor. The Tower provided hundreds of jobs, made millions in revenue, and made every person who walked through its doors happy, that was, until thousands died in the firestorm that took it down.

The attack also created an infectious toxin that the media nicknamed Tower Toxin which spread through the air and killed people in a similar fashion to radiation poisoning.

Obviously, what happened to the tower left the city devastated, but to make matters worse, the group reached out to the highest-rated reporter, Rebecca Whales, a few days after the blast and through her, they claimed to be crusaders intent on bringing America back to the simple family values that the country was built on.

They explained that they blamed the Carlton Tower for encouraging wasteful spending, greed, vanity, and ultimately destroying the wholesomeness they were working to protect and they felt that bombing the Carlton Tower was the only way to impassion people enough to make real changes in society. The Brotherhood also threatened more attacks if they didn't see some change immediately.

Firestone had a persistent gut feeling that the narrative in the news did not fit the actual evidence in front of him and that feeling kept him investigating objectively.

Firestone learned that a man named Martin Corrocco was working to sell the Carlton Tower without his wife's consent and the lady, who had hired Scarleto to kill her husband to stop the sale, was so deeply disturbed by the large-scale loss of life that she ultimately broke down when Firestone confronted her in the interrogation room and confirmed that the bombing was another one of Scarleto's overcomplicated plots.

Because that critical interview confirmed Scarleto's involvement, Firestone took some questionable initiative and had his personal friend and go-to Cyber specialist, Angelique Marceau, activate a satellite tracking beacon that Agent Leah Fong had clandestinely planted in Scarleto's cell phone during their nearly-fatal death match eleven years earlier.

Firestone followed the beacon and he found the two terrorists that remained at large after the Carlton Tower investigation was completed, but to Firestone's fury, Scarleto and the terrorists escaped on Scarleto's same plane.

Worse, was the fact that the beacon was supposed to be reserved for yet another take-down operation targeting Scarleto, but because Firestone had used the beacon, that operation could not happen.

Firestone's decision to compromise that operation was about to cost him his career, when a call came in to FBI Director Dwayne Meyer explaining that Firestone's partner Leah Fong had gone missing.

Special Agent Leah Fong had gone missing while investigating a Chinese gang called the Golden Dragons. The Dragons were part of a Triad: in this case it meant three gangs working as one toward a common goal, but they used the name 'Triad' to intimidate potential federal informants into believing they were affiliated with the long-established Chinese Syndicate with international outreach.

In the case of Leah's mission, this Triad was suspected of human trafficking, which automatically suggested a connection to Scarleto and the Scarlet Orchid.

Leah was chosen for the op because of her Chinese heritage and her history with Scarleto and similar cases. Firestone knew that Leah was too good of an officer and too perfect of casting to be blown and disappear in the 'traditional' fashion. Firestone believed that Scarleto had a hand in Leah's disappearance as a twisted method of revenge for Firestone almost catching him a second time.

Director Meyer agreed and felt that there was no one more qualified than Firestone to retrieve Leah, so Meyer and Firestone composed a taskforce and scripted the undercover operation Firestone was working.

The new taskforce consisted of Detective Donna Sparks, Sparks' Captain Montgomery Snowden, Forensic Scientist Dawson Sour, and Cyber Specialist Angelique Marceau.

Sparks was Meyer's pick for this operation, but Firestone agreed without a complaint because Sparks was essential to Firestone successfully uncovering the truth behind what happened to the Carlton Tower because she was a damn good detective with a never-give-up spirit. Sparks also had plenty of skin in the game against Scarleto and the remaining two terrorists because her team had been killed when they raided the bomber's booby-trapped workshop the day that the Tower fell.

Sparks also blended in a little better physically with the almost completely Asian migrant community that they had to go undercover in because she was shorter in height and had an exotic Israeli complexion.

Sparks recommended Dawson Sour for the team because he was apparently essential to her producing winning forensic results to Firestone and, with two of his major players involved, Snowden insisted he be part of it also.

Angelique Marceau was Firestone's pick, but everyone else agreed immediately and with the team together, Leah's rescue was in full swing.

Unfortunately, pulling together the details of the rescue operation took months.

During those months, Firestone had no way of knowing what was happening to Leah or if she was even still alive to be rescued.

Firestone knew that his mind needed to be *here*, but his memories were so vivid that he thought he could smell the cordite from the gunshots, the smoke from the burning school, and the smoke from the smoldering Tower. He choked slightly on the memory of the African dust, he heard fragments of voices and ear-bending screams, and every time he thought about Leah, he sunk deeper into his mental 3D movie.

His memories were turning his hatred for Scarleto into *obsession* and that obsession was clouding his judgement. He was focussed on why Scarleto needed to be stopped and not on what he needed to do to stop him. Snowden saw that inner struggle on their car's camera and decided to do something about it, "Remember people," Snowden authoritatively said into the microphone connected to Firestone and Sparks' earpieces, "Your mission is to follow the path that Leah took in the hopes of finding her and hopefully finding Scarleto with her. If you get Scarleto back in your sights, your orders are to capture Scarleto and interrogate him with the intention of tearing down what's left of the Scarlet Orchid if possible and kill him if capture isn't a safe certainty."

"Yes, we will," Firestone said. Snowden restating the mission got Firestone out of own head because they helped remind him that he was not alone in his demand to see this mission completed. Firestone began to pay attention to his surroundings with renewed focus just in time for him and Sparks to exit their unmarked federal SUV outside the same Chinese restaurant where Special Agent Leah Fong had begun her clandestine mission nearly seven months ago.

The restaurant was in the heart of The Asian Quarter; a traditional and multicultural Asian Theme Park. The park's theme of ninjas and dragons was emphasised by spine-tingling themed rides, captivating games, and daily and nightly parades that included fireworks, but a very real and beautiful Asian community blossomed around the park also.

Snowden worried about all of the traditional Asian beauty around them because Firestone and Sparks stuck out like neon at midnight amidst it.

Firestone was six-foot-two-inches tall which had him towering over most of the locals. He had fair skin and slowly greying brown hair that was fluffed into a contemporary style and his soulful and mission-focussed brown eyes were hidden behind black sunglasses that looked almost too big for his thin face. The glasses were feeding video to Marceau and Snowden, but they also fed Firestone's general celebrity appeal that was turning the ladies' heads instead of camouflaging him.

Detective Donna Sparks had her hair tied in a long brown braid and she was wearing a biker outfit that coordinated with Firestone's overall look, but she seemed too much like an undercover cop because her movements were stiff.

Snowden knew that she was struggling because she was putting real effort into copying Firestone instead of moving freely and Snowden felt he had to correct her.

"Relax Donna," Snowden warned, "You're just a biker chick going to lunch with her boyfriend…" Sparks inconspicuously nodded, swallowed, and calmed herself.

Angelique chuckled once Snowden released the talk button on the microphone and Snowden looked at her and she casually explained, "You are a great Captain, but you do not have to worry. Tony is bold, but he cares about this mission and Donna may seem out of her element, but she is a good officer and she will adapt if she needs to."

Angelique was raised on the Caribbean Island of St. Marie. She was about three-hundred-fifty pounds overweight and sported a modern punk style where high-fashion clothes met discreet red and gold streaks in her extremely curly hair that were a bold but beautiful change from the pink and purple ones she had always had.

Angelique also loved loud nail polish and bright makeup, but even despite her weight and unique style, she was a dark beauty whose accent clung to her first language of French.

She had a knowledgeable, motherly, and incredibly attractive mystique that encouraged Snowden to agree with her judge of character and relax slightly.

Snowden was Angelique's physical opposite. He had the same looks and vibe of a lone ranger from a classic western, except he was squished into an up-to-date boss-man's suit.

Snowden was used to being the overly-protective and highly respected boss, but he and his people had been largely left in the dark about how things would go down and both Firestone and Sparks seemed unprepared. He was uncomfortable with the situation, but there was nothing he could do except trust Angelique, so he silenced his leadership qualities in favor of letting the events of the operation play out, but it was no Sunday drive simply watching.

Firestone hustled Sparks into a table near the back of the restaurant. They sat there, people watching, for a few seconds until Sparks' anxiety reached a critical level and she asked, "What do we do now? Are we meeting someone?"

Firestone sat back and smiled at Sparks. "No, we're not going to get anywhere by asking 'have you seen this cop whose cover is in question around?' or 'how does one become part of the Triad'?"

Sparks looked around nervously, "Shhh!" she said, "Anyone in this restaurant could be working for a gang. You could blow our cover."

"Exactly." He said proudly.

"What the hell is this?" Snowden asked Angelique as his anger and anxiety grew. Angelique settled him as best she could and they both watched intently.

Sparks' face scrunched with confusion.

"Hey, what's a guy got to do to get some Spicy Noodles in this joint?" Firestone shouted with a staged drunken lilt to his voice.

Sparks was extremely shocked and desperately tried to shut him down because she was unaware of how their operation was supposed to work, but Firestone left Sparks in the dark on purpose, hoping for that reaction. Getting what he wanted inspired him to turn up the heat and he began rudely obstructing bustling staff.

In a matter of what seemed like seconds, a clearly gang-affiliated group of men entered the restaurant and the nervous elderly hostess pointed the gangsters to Firestone's table.

Firestone and Sparks both recognized the gangsters from their pre-mission briefing. The leader of the group was Jacko Chang, leader by birthright of the Golden Dragons and the men around him were low-level enforcers. Everyone was surprised to see

Chang working a low-level restaurant rough-up, but whoever the players were didn't change the game.

"I'm sorry you two, but we need you to leave," Jacko said civilly.

"Not until I get my Spicy Noodles, Jacko-ass" Firestone stated boldly. As he spoke, he assumed a dominant stance putting his chest right against Chang's.

Chang and Firestone stood deadlocked for a long moment. Many of the spectators chuckled at Firestone's antics and name-calling; others understood the pressure of the moment and coward as they planned their escapes. Sparks simply sat there. She was trapped in the moment between drawing her gun and letting Firestone finish whatever it was that he was doing.

Suddenly, Firestone's house of cards fell. Chang punched Firestone and sent him flying across his table which sent water glasses and menus flying to the floor with him. Sparks and Firestone were both stunned by the power of the punch Chang was able to deliver with bandaged knuckles and, because of her shock, Sparks lost her chance to pull out her gun before Chang's enforcers had her in a strong chokehold.

Firestone and Sparks were muscled out and as they were dragged away, the visual and audio feed they were giving Marceau and Snowden faded into white noise. Snowden and Marceau were sent into a panic, but there was nothing they could do except dispatch the local police and wait.

It was unfortunate that Firestone and Sparks had to be captured at that moment because the circumstances left them unable stop the Brotherhood's second strike.

Chapter 2

Much earlier that same day, before the members of the taskforce searching for him were even awake, Pierre Mambossa was intently focussed on his latest project.

Beads of sweat crawled annoyingly slowly down the sides of his face. After a moment, he paused briefly to wipe his face and admire his work so far. He had put his heart and soul into converting the antique pocket watch that Scarleto had provided him with into his latest bomb and he wasn't willing to let his own moisture damage it.

Mambossa, Scarleto, and infamous hit man John Murphy Bell were the last survivors of the criminal group responsible for bringing down the Carlton Tower. Mambossa had received word that the officers most eager to bring him to justice were staging an undercover mission mere blocks from where he was. He knew that they knew his identity and that they were looking for Special Agent Leah Fong who was imprisoned in the closet that was steps behind his work station. Mambossa loved dancing with danger because it gave him the feeling of being in control and having the upper hand over the agent gave him that feeling for the first time in a long time.

The day that Mambossa and his associates brought down the Carlton Tower, it was packed to capacity; holiday shoppers were taking advantage of the year-end clearances, the medical and business offices were running in those days between

Christmas and New Years, and the Corrocco Casino was hosting a holiday gala as well as the clandestine sale of the entire tower.

Mambossa didn't usually accept team assignments because he was so addicted to control, but he was in desperate need of cash when Scarleto found him and asked him to assist in the Tower's destruction, so he agreed to it. The team aspect, however, gave the control that Mambossa craved over to Bell.

Mambossa was told that he and his team were assigned to assassinate a particular target in the Corrocco Casino, but as the explosives expert and wheelman, Mambossa restricted his focus to the areas he had control over in effort to keep as much control as possible.

He made a high-end briefcase bomb that hid the murder of the target easily and wired a car bomb to blow the tower's foundation.

The car bomb was a bigger challenge than the briefcase device because the foundation of the Carlton Tower was designed to withstand explosive car accidents, but he was still successful because he parked the converted suburban vehicle in the underground parking lot next to what was probably the only structural foundation post that would have weakened the tower's foundation enough to affect the building.

Although he was not there to see it in person because he had to be ready and waiting to the drive the getaway vehicle from a few blocks away, it thrilled him to hear that both bombs had preformed even better than he had anticipated.

Ultimately, his devices had killed many thousands of people, so he had done his job well and his success almost made him proud enough to cease his hatred, but his team killed any sense of pride.

There were four other members of Mambossa's team; Jonathan Murphy Bell, Kin Luk, Jeanine Sing, and Delia Horsoff.

Apparently, Jeanine Sing had been killed when one of their target's security guards shot her just prior to the bombings,

Delia Horsoff had died as a result of being too close to his briefcase bomb when it was detonated, and Kin Luk killed himself a few days after they escaped the blast site. Before he killed himself however, Kin Luk wrote a tell-all suicide note that exposed the team and their mission.

Luk's suicide note put the police hot on Mambossa's and Bell's trails and cut Scarleto's resources down significantly. Fortunately, Scarleto still had a private plane and a loyal flight crew which the three of them utilized to make a narrow escape. Scarleto also kidnapped Agent Fong with the hope of giving them an emergency ace to play.

Mambossa hated being bounced around as he and Scarleto avoided law enforcement while the heat was on. He hated being stuffed onto a plane and flown somewhere he had no say in, but he knew that they needed to spend several weeks on the nameless-map-dot of an island in the Pacific Ocean while their escape plane was completely detailed and the leads on them evaporated, so he had no control for months on end. Agent Fong also made their getaway difficult because she was always struggling to escape and screaming non-stop.

According to the news that Mambossa did hear upon landing, approximately three-hundred-thousand people had been killed as a result of the Carlton Tower disaster. Mambossa knew that many of the causalities died due to his artistry and others died from a unique infection that was unintentionally created. Apparently, the toxin was a result of a variety of chemicals and materials within the tower melting and reacting together during the blast.

Mambossa was able to avoid the toxin thanks the distance his car was from the blast and limited length of time he spent near people exposed to the toxin, but he always felt that there were gaps in the spotty news coverage that he was able to get.

Mambossa hated surprises like the toxin and he hated not knowing whether he could revel in his success or dread that hated surprise; with the spotty coverage, he could never be sure, but all of that was back in December and January.

It was now near the end of April and more than just the news cycle had changed in that time. Mambossa, Scarleto, and Bell eventually circled back in March to find a city that was rapidly rebuilding triumphantly while Scarleto had hoped to keep it permanently strangled by fear.

To Amilio Scarleto's surprise, an old enemy, Special Agent Anthony Firestone, was the nations hero and Firestone's boss Director Dwayne Meyer, was insultingly calling Scarleto's bluff.

In a single press conference, Director Meyer called their group 'a collection of low-IQ bearing individuals pretending to be driven by higher calling when they were actually spineless, tactless murderers-for-hire.'

What irked Scarleto the most was the fact that, for the most part, Director Meyer's insults were accurate, but an insane Scarleto still believed the world still believed in the terrorist organisation that they had faked. Scarleto intended to make Director Meyer and his team of heroic investigators into fools.

Scarleto's original plan was to strap a bomb to Leah and use her to blow up Meyer's and Firestone's FBI field office. The risk involved in that plan was what prompted Scarleto to make this under-the-radar sweatshop Laundromat into his new base of operations for their strike, but the excessive body heat, the heat from the illegal venting of the washers and dryers, and the warmth of the spring sunshine blasting through the window he was facing made the working conditions almost unbearable for Mambossa who also struggled with the noise of the machines and the staff.

The workers yelled to be heard over the machines and they yelled in a misguided effort to seal the language barrier between staff members. The conditions made it difficult to focus, but Mambossa's life depended on his focus.

Mambossa hated the conditions here, but the proximity to the taskforce that was hunting him was the only thing giving him that all-important rush that drove him to continue on this path.

Then he gave things a second thought; being so close to the taskforce that was hunting him wasn't the only exciting thing, the fact the plan to turn Leah into a human bomb had changed and no one but he and Scarleto knew about the change in plans was also thrilling. He was also the team's leader now and the thought of leadership excited him also.

After his relatively lengthy break for reflection, cooling, and wiping; Mambossa attempted to return to work. Using a pair of fine-tip pliers, he strategically weaved a small bluish-green wire, hardly thicker than a strand of human hair, through the gears of the watch to touch a similar red wire that had been weaved through the inner workings of the watch from the other side.

Satisfied he'd brought the bluish-green wire close enough to the red one, he breathed carefully and exchanged the fine-tip pliers for an antique surgical clamp he kept in his tool kit. He then used that clamp to crimp the tips of each wire so that they stood erect in mirroring 'L' shapes.

Once the wires were firmly in the shape he needed them, he began crafting the foil carriage that would hold his custom-made blasting cap in place. The foil carriage would funnel the power from the wires into the cap and funnel the concussive force of the exploding cap back down the battered wire to wear it would strike the fuse. The fuse would then ignite the explosive between the inner mechanisms of the watch bomb, making it explode. Mambossa also needed the foil carriage to hold some special magnetic lettering lead that would ensure this bomb literally sent a message.

After using his surgical clamp to tighten the foil to the wires, he laid his blasting cap in the crudely prepared foil nest and returned the clamp to his tool bag. He then leaned back in his chair, pulled his magnetising jeweller's goggles that he had been wearing up on to his forehead, and rubbed his exhausted eyes profusely.

As he rubbed, he heard a familiar thumping on the wall behind him. Mambossa knew the noise was Jacko Chang, leader of the Golden Dragons, roughing up special Agent Leah Fong again.

Fong was not only Agent Firestone's partner and she was also the person Agent Firestone loved most in the world. Scarleto believed that killing her would be the ultimate blow to the FBI, however, Scarleto enjoyed playing head games with Firestone and Fong too much to simply let her go.

In fact, Scarleto intentionally planned their team's attack on the Carlton Tower for when Agent Fong was working undercover with Chang's gang because Scarleto had a long-standing relationship with the Dragons and he knew he could manipulate them into keeping Agent Fong hostage as another head game.

Scarleto's thinking was that Agent Firestone would be so focussed on his partner's absence that he and his group could fly under the radar, but Firestone proved to be a formidable opponent without his partner.

Scarleto still decided to take his and Firestone's game of cat and mouse to the next level. Scarleto revealed Fong's identity as an agent to the gangs that she found herself in the paths of and offered each of the gang leaders an opportunity to try and torture her for information. Scarleto's only condition was that they leave her alive and in his custody for his master plan and they agreed.

For months, dozens of Asian gangsters had been periodically seeking them out and taking advantage of Scarleto's offer to press Agent Fong for information.

Jacko Chang came most often though because Fong had been dating him as part of her cover. The information she had was closest to his heart and his gang.

Just as Mambossa straightened up, intending to return to work again, Chang left Fong's stockade and the two men locked eyes.

Mambossa found Chang more frightening than Scarleto because while Scarleto would be considered elderly and was crippled by a tremendous set of injuries Agents Fong and Firestone had saddled him with over the years; Chang had only just turned forty and had the atheism of a man half his age.

Chang was taller and bulkier than any other Dragon member and he was gifted at every form of martial arts from the most ancient and traditional to the most modern. Chang was talented with every weapon and never backed down from any challenge, whether it was fighting or business.

Scarleto's methods were often out of date and tactless. He was more likely to walk away submissively and then have someone else kill you later while Chang could make a man afraid to even hold his gaze.

More than that, Scarleto had a bushy, fattened, and almost fatherly look to him while Chang always inspired fear. At that moment, as he stared Mambossa down with his hands still dripping with Agent Fong's blood, Mambossa realized that Chang was empty inside. Agent Fong had clearly broken his heart and more-than-likely destroyed his empire by making his gang lose faith and respect for him because he let a cop get so close.

Chang was now a target for the people he once considered family and was an even greater target for rival gangs. He had nothing left to lose.

In that moment, Mambossa worried that Chang may not have been satisfied with attacking Leah Fong and may have come for him also, but the men only traded respectful nods and Chang left. Mambossa breathed heavily for a second before returning to work.

This next phase of his project was the most crucial and dangerous part of his craft. For this portion, he was using a modified culinary torch to put a final seal on the carriage for the blasting cap. The seal would permanently attach the foil nest to the wires and encapsulate the blasting cap so its energy wouldn't go anywhere but where it would be needed to ignite the explosive. The seal would also make the device virtually impossible to diffuse.

He began to calm slightly as the torch was working well. The foil melted to wires with ease, so he began to swish the torch over the fold that now covered the blasting cap relatively carelessly.

Suddenly, a spine-tinglingly-annoying sound violently disrupted his concentration. The disruption caused him to jump in his seat and jostle the burning torch and his awkward movements caused the torch to burn through the foil nest which created a cascade reaction that Mambossa was powerless to stop.

The foil carriage caved in on itself at the point where the torch had burned it and the bend that was created allowed the two volatile wire tips to touch the blasting cap at each end. In a split second, a deadly circuit was completed and the cap and the wires sparked.

Mambossa had not yet connected the explosives, but the popping of the burning wires and blasting cap were more deafening than rifle shots and they reignited his anger. Mambossa pushed back from his work table so aggressively that his chair tipped. It was uncomfortable being stuck like a flipped turtle when he was so angry.

Each pop was the sound of months of work burning to ash, and because he was stuck on his back until the chaos settled, he let himself focus on the fact that the annoyance that caused this destruction was the raspy cough of the one man he hated most in the world, John Murphy Bell.

Mambossa hated Bell for many reasons. First, Bell lied about who he was; he said his name was Eric Bell when it was actually John Murphy Bell and in Mambossa's culture a man's name is tied to his soul and lies of any kind, especially about a name, carry the highest dishonor.

Second, Bell undersold the risk the team would be taking at the Carlton Tower. He told them that the Carlton Tower assassination would be an easy job and because they went in expecting ease, the other team members died and Mambossa came frighteningly close to doing the same when of Bell's arrogance resulted in a shootout with Agent Firestone.

Back at the Carlton Tower, Bell became infected with the Tower Toxin and sustained some minor injuries in addition to breaking his ankle. When his ankle broke, Bell treated it with quick-fix field medicine he learned in the army and strong pain killing pills.

The pills clouded Bell's judgement and his clouded judgement led him into a trap that reporter Rebecca Whales had set which allowed the FBI to close in on them. FBI Agent Firestone got so close to catching them, in fact, that he managed to shoot Bell while he stood on the steps of his escape plane.

Bell's bullet wounds, the Tower Toxin, and the poor treatment of his ankle combined and left him terminally septic. He wasn't long for the world, but knowing that Bell would die soon did not make his presence or his incessant coughing any less tolerable in Mambossa's opinion.

Once the popping stopped, Mambossa stood and began to assess the damage. Mambossa was still assessing when Scarleto ran down.

Scarleto was clearly flustered and angry as he asked, "What the hell is going on? I don't intend to die today, kiddo."

Mambossa was too angry to say what exactly was on his mind, but he pointed to Bell and said, "It was him..." He breathed a heavy sigh, relaxed slightly, and continued, "To do this kind of work, I must focus intently and his coughing breaks that focus. When I cannot focus properly, I make mistakes and things get wrecked."

Scarleto panicked and quickly inserted himself directly in front of the watch bomb so that Mambossa was crowded out, "Can it be fixed?"

"I believe so," Mambossa said as he pushed Scarleto aside so he could finish his damage assessment, "but it will not be as reliable as it would have been had this accident not happened. We should place it closer to the stage in order to ensure we get what we need..."

"That will be difficult, but I can arrange it." Scarleto turned and started back up the steps, but Mambossa wasn't finished.

"Why don't we just kill Bell now?" Mambossa asked somberly. After a minute, he elaborated, "I am willing to deliver the watch. We don't need him to do it and I can't guarantee I will have it finished on time with him here to distract me."

Scarleto walked back down and put a bracing hand on Mambossa's shoulder as he explained, "I need you in the future and I don't need Bell. We follow the plan as we planned it; Bell will make the delivery. Do your job, do it well, and get it done tonight. It has to be done tonight." Scarleto pressurized his bracing hand, forcing Mambossa to sit back down at his work table.

Mambossa nodded and got back to work. *"Tonight"* Mambossa whispered to himself, "*In a few more hours, I will be free of Bell and I will be a king once more.*"

Mambossa was not satisfied with Scarleto's selfish plan however. Mambossa decided then and there that he would kill himself and end Scarleto's oppression, but he knew he had to do that in a meaningful way.

Reporter Rebecca Whales would have to immortalize him.

Chapter 3

That warm spring day faded into the perfect evening for an opera before Bell felt ready for it. Bell moved with the speed and grace of a man more than twice his age. He hobbled into the packed Sapphire Theatre with the assistance of a department store walker and handed his ticket to the hostess before she helped him to his seat.

Had the circumstances behind tonight been different, Bell would have revelled in the opulence around him. He had the edge seat of the center column of seats three rows back from the stage. From that seat, he could see the orchestra settling in to the pit below the stage, he saw the ruffles of the curtain as the cast and crew hustled to pull everything together before the curtain rose and he could see the ornate leafing on the balconies above him, but even with all of that distracting amazement holding his gaze, he could not ignore the painted and textured ceiling that could have been painted by Michael Angelo.

Bell slid his sweaty palms along the soft red velvet of his seat. He thought to himself, *'if I have to die in a chair, I'm glad it's this one.'*

Bell felt his silky blue suit under his sweaty fingers. It bothered him that the last clothes he would ever wear had to be this silk suit that looked like it was pulled from the prom section back in the '70's, but because he had been so foolish in their previous mission, his team was no longer giving him any choice.

Bell used to pride himself on how he dressed and groomed for his murders. He used to tailor his image so that he could become whoever he needed to be to get close to victim and then blend into the rest of the crowd once the killing was done. His mission was to murder and then disappear; he was supposed to never be noticed and always be forgotten. For this job however, it was going to be impossible for anyone to forget him.

His suit was unforgettable and so was his hair style. His internal infection and injuries had left him with many scars and bald patches, so Scarleto had forced him to fill in his scalp with a cheaply-made hair piece that wasn't quite the correct shade of brown and Bell's newly-developed sensitivity to light left him needing purple-tinted sunglasses.

Because he was doomed, Bell hadn't bothered to shave in the past three days, but the skin of his face was about as bad as his scalp so he looked like hell. The walker he needed also helped draw attention to his suffering.

His goal had always been to be a spider catching flies in shadows, but his purpose here was to be noticed; here, he was a message. Still, knowing that he was meant to be memorable did not make him comfortable with it.

Bell became absorbed in self-reflection. He thought about all of the things he wished he had said, all of the things he wished he could still do, and everything he wished he could do differently. He thought of all of the women he wished he kissed. Tears welled in his eyes as he wished he had been a different man and he wished he could tell his mom how he felt.

Bell was so soaked in his own regrets that he hadn't noticed the lights dim and the curtain lift. He numbly squirmed through the initial opening of the opera, but his attention lifted with the first solo song. The lead soprano was singing a sorrowful solo with a cold and dark funeral scene behind her. He didn't speak Italian, but he felt like that rose-haired Diva was singing right into God's ears and asking on his behalf forgiveness.

He barely had the strength to remove the antique pocket watch from the silken inner pocket of his jacket, but he did.

Bell saw the hands of the watch stop in his palm and took a slow saddened breath and whispered, *"Damn it"* as he realised he couldn't change anything. The last thing Bell ever saw was a painfully-bright white flash as the watch bomb Mambossa had made exploded in his palm, and then he was gone.

Chapter 4

Firestone had lost all sense of feeling in his body as he drove that evening. Needless to say, things had not gone as they were scripted to. Earlier that morning, Firestone's plan had been to boldly weasel his way into becoming a new low-level enforcer for the Triad that was working in the Asian Quarter, but back at the restaurant where the operation began, Jacko Chang came to collect them and Chang was no fool.

Firestone was supposed to aggravate the enforcer into beating him up. Detective Sparks would then beg the enforcer for forgiveness and barter their non-existent biker gang's mythical drug supply and cross-border transportation for Firestone's freedom. If the gang was interested, they would eventually learn the inner workings of the gang which would include what had happened to Leah and Scarleto's involvement.

They would then be able to use what they learned to complete Leah's mission and take down both the Scarlet Orchid and the Golden Dragons, but Chang was no dumb enforcer.

Chang saw through Firestone and Sparks' facade immediately and brought them down to his basement office via a prohibition era tunnel stemming from the center of the restaurant floor.

Chang had held on to the prohibition era glamour with his decorative choices. The furniture was antique and ornate, the lighting was crystalline, the floor was tastefully covered in Persian rugs, and all of the walls had auburn wide-board paneling, but it was difficult to appreciate the preserved history surrounding them when Chang and his bruisers had them on their knees with their hands zip-tied behind their backs.

"Alright, what are you two supposed to be?" Chang asked. As he spoke, he slid comfortably into his domineering desk. "At first, I thought you two were idiot tourists who had too much to drink and were digging for a gangster experience in your drunken stupor, but then you got all up in my face and I picked up on some things."

Sparks and Firestone squirmed angrily, but they had no choice but to keep listening, "Foremost was the fact that there wasn't even a whisper of liquor on your breath, so my initial assessment of you was obviously flawed. Then, your girl over there reached to her hip when things started to get uncomfortable and, in my experience, biker chicks rarely carry. They mostly rely on their men to rise to a challenge. Also, I doubt that any self-respecting biker gang would let you leave your houses dressed in that set-dressing..."

"So, if you're not tourists and you're not bikers, you must be cops; am I right?" Chang rose slowly, walked in front of his desk, fanned out across it, and started fondling Firestone's wired sunglasses. "That certainly explains why you held on to these with such a death-grip once I punched you; are they meant to signal the Calvary?"

"If their purpose is to call for help, you're going to be disappointed because this passageway may have been built in the times of prohibition and refurbished to look untouched since then, but it has been rigged to block Wi-Fi, satellite, radio, and cellular signals. The last thing your people witnessed was me doing nothing wrong; I merely punched and forcefully escorted out an irritating presence from my restaurant before a wave of white-noise killed their visuals and their audio."

"No one knows where you are and even if a team raids the restaurant, the odds of them finding you down here in this web of dark anti-tech tunnels and hidden doorways before I kill you and escape are frighteningly slim, so why don't you two stop insulting our intelligence," Chang did a wide-armed gesture that was meant to include all of the gangsters in the room, "and tell us who you are and what you're doing here. If we like your answers, we'll let you go and we can forget this ever happened."

Detective Sparks straightened up her posture. She was clearly tight-lipped and probably willing to die a slow death before saying anything. Firestone admired that and, for a long moment, he was right there with her; caught between staying silent or throwing out a clever denial. Then a risky thought swept in and consumed his mind; he acted on that thought, "I'm an FBI Special Agent and I'm looking for Amilio Scarleto."

Chang slowly walked over and knelt so that his eyes were once again level with Firestone's. He flashed a wicked smile and said, "You're Anthony, aren't you; Leah's partner?" Firestone couldn't hide his anger at Chang using Leah's name and Chang laughed at him. Chang cupped Firestone's ear in his hand and shook Firestone's head with his grip.

Chang got up and turned his back to them. Chang's posture slumped and his voice hollowed, "Leah loves you, you know? She called me by your name once or twice; when I made her laugh and as she fell asleep after we made love..." Firestone thought he heard a tear in Chang's voice.

"At first, I thought you were a boyfriend she couldn't get over and I hoped I could make her forget you, but when I learned you were her partner, I realised that you were always going to be a part of her..."

Chang turned back to them with fury in his eyes, "I suppose that honour is deserved because you seem willing to die to find her..."

At that moment, the building shook and they were showered in dust. Chang's attention turned to what had happened and he and his enforcers surfaced, leaving Firestone and Sparks alone to attempt escape.

Sparks and Firestone squirmed until the zip-ties trapping their hands broke. They then found their weapons in Chang's desk and grabbed Firestone's spy glasses before following the sound of Chang and the rest of the gang through the web of tunnels. Unfortunately, they met Chang and the enforcers on the steps that they needed to take to get up to the restaurant. The group ended up in a tense standoff.

Everyone except Chang drew their weapons, but Chang raised his hands in a disarming fashion and said, "Please, we need your help." He then convinced his men to lower their weapons.

Sparks and Firestone's curiosity got the better of them and they let Chang lead them back to his office to explain his plea.

"Scarleto approached me a few months ago. He showed me photos of Leah working as an agent and he explained her mission to me." Chang was flustered, but Firestone felt in control of his own emotions and the situation, so he patiently listened, "I lead the Golden Dragons, but the organization is vast and I only took it over from my father relatively recently, so I am not involved in the day to day very often and I do not know everything."

"I did not think that we dabbled in human trafficking, but when the truth about Leah came to light, I searched it out."

"At first I was angry with Leah for lying so consistently, and then I became anxious about potentially going to prison because of Leah..." Chang emotionally studied his bandaged hands and then spoke sorrowfully, "I regretfully admit that I took out my anger and angst on Leah and I stood by and did nothing as others with grudges against her did the same."

Firestone felt his bearings unhinging, "Is she dead?"

Chang shook his head. *Leah was alive.* Chang continued before for Firestone could ask more questions, "But after a while, I wondered who Scarleto was and I wondered why he would expose Leah only to demand that she live? What did Scarleto have to gain from exposing Leah?"

"My curiosity caused me to dig deeper into Scarleto, his organization, and my organization. I learned that the human trafficking element was forced on us back when my father led the gang."

"Back then, we were in the midst of a territorial war and we were losing more product and people than we were pillaging. At our lowest point, Scarleto approached us and offered to use his resources to help us win the war on the condition that we trade him our resources to use for his human trafficking railroad."

"Because he felt he had no other choice, my father agreed to Scarleto's trade, but we learned later that Scarleto had staged the entire gang war as a method of building up his operation; we were forced into the human trafficking by Scarleto and he wouldn't let us leave his hold alive."

"I grasped that Leah would have come to that conclusion as well eventually and when I came to that realization, I also realized that Scarleto had sold Leah out to protect his own ass. He ripped my life apart and expected to deceive me into believing I was in his debt."

"Last night, I confronted him and when we argued, I noticed some plans that looked like he intended to blow up your FBI headquarters, so I threatened to release Leah and warn her of his plans if he didn't break down his human trafficking operation and leave Dragon territory forever."

"He laughed in my face and started spouting lies about how both of our organizations benefitted from working together. I became so enraged that I pulled a gun on him and escorted him out at gunpoint. He swore up and down to me that I would regret making an enemy of him, but the next morning, he returned and apologized for his behaviour."

"I believed his organization was struggling, so I let him in and let him know that I owned him. I reasoned that he would understand the power that we held over him, but I had also heard the stories of his unpredictability, so I got Leah's help."

Firestone perked up.

"I made it appear as though she was undergoing another torture session while I told her *everything*. I told her about all of the criminality within my organization; some I was party to, the rest I didn't know about until Scarleto inspired me to find it. I also told her about Scarleto's plans for the headquarters bombing."

"She said she could use the information I had given her to help if she could get to you and the rest of her team. I believed her, so I helped her hide in a ventilation shaft in the roof of room she was being held in. To my knowledge, she is still there.

"My plan was for the next torturer to assume that Leah had escaped and her apparent disappearance would send Scarleto into a tailspin. I had hoped to smuggle Leah out in the ensuing chaos, but some circumstances have changed."

Firestone's heart was pounding so loudly in his ears that he barely heard Chang explain, "I don't know what happened; perhaps Scarleto was serious about how deeply my anger had offended him, perhaps he felt his plans to bomb the FBI were too risky, or perhaps those plans were a misdirect from the start, but that earthquake we just felt was the shockwave from an explosion at the Sapphire Theatre."

"My mother was attending the opera playing at the Sapphire tonight. Scarleto knew this because she invited him to attend with her. I'm confident he revised his plan to attack the FBI to attack the theatre instead because I saw his bomber working on one small bomb. I doubt Scarleto has the resources to carry out two attacks, the FBI must be safe for now, but I don't know if my mother is safe or not."

"Scarleto has since aligned himself with my former second in command and it appears they have revised Scarleto's attack plan to hurt me and now I want to hurt him."

"Most of my old gang is loyal to Scarleto and my old friend Lee Wu now, but these men our loyal to me. We are planning to sacrifice our lives in the defense of the legacy that my father left. In death, we will make the name The Golden Dragons mean something worthwhile again, but the gang will fall."

"For our sacrifice to mean what we need it to mean, Scarleto must fall as well so I'll take you to Scarleto's base of operations. I'll give you all that Scarleto has, including Leah and while I'm in jail, owning up for all that I've done, they will keep the other Dragons out of your way."

"We can't condone gang violence..." Sparks whispered.

One of the enforcers behind Chang stepped up and said, "We're not giving you a choice."

Firestone and Sparks recognized that they were outnumbered and outgunned, so they justified accepting Chang's terms as a unique way to call for backup. Now, they were closely following Chang in a car that he had rented them.

Firestone was numbed by dozens of emotions hitting him at once; *was this an elaborate trap set by Scarleto and Chang? Would Leah be on the other side of this drive? What would she do when she saw him? Would she love him like Chang suggested or would she hate him for taking so long to rescue her? What if Chang was wrong about Leah's whereabouts and Scarleto had involved her in his latest bombing?*

Firestone glanced over at the billowing smoke breaking the star-coated night sky. The Sapphire Theatre had definitely been struck, but was Scarleto truly behind it? If it was Scarleto, was Chang right about what motivated it?

Suddenly, Sparks pulled Firestone's attention back to reality by saying, "We're here, Tony."

Firestone slowed to a stop and parked in the gritty lot of the rundown Laundromat.

Firestone jogged through the building, paying no attention to the illegal workers swarming the room. Eventually, Chang guided Firestone to yet another prohibition tunnel which led down to pit of a basement.

The room shared the decor and auburn aura of Chang's office but the basement was devoid of furniture and had an obstructive web of vents and plumbing at its ceiling.

Firestone noticed a polished board resting on two sawhorses and a decorator's bench pulled under, making a hastily-pulled-together work station underneath a rotting window. There was a war era work-lamp on the corner and jeweller's tools thrown carelessly about the 'tabletop'.

It was clearly the bomber's work station and in the center of the mess, written in bold blue paint were the words: *'you called us gutless and dumb, you were wrong. Long live the Brotherhood; long live our pure America.'* Firestone ran his fingers over the letters in a careless daze and because he was so distracted by the bomber's message, Firestone didn't notice Chang disappear around a large pillar and unlock Leah from a closet cut into it.

"Hello, Tony." Leah's voice caught his attention immediately. He spun on his heels and stared her down in tearful disbelief.

She was bruised, bloodied, and in desperate need of a shower. She looked like she had lost weight that she couldn't afford to lose and she was crying a little. Still, he ran up and hugged her like he had the night before she left for her mission so long ago. She hugged him back and kissed his cheek softly, "I'm so glad you're alive, I'm so sorry." Firestone said.

"It was really bad," Leah whispered, "But I got what I came for." She then backed out of Firestone's arms.

"Are you Agent Fong?" Sparks asked as she walked down the stairs to finally join them in the basement after being temporarily lost in the bustle of the upper level. Firestone was embarrassed for having distanced himself from Sparks without knowing it as soon as he'd parked; Leah nodded and Sparks added, "Where's Chang?" For the first time since they were grabbed at his restaurant, Firestone recognized that he had lost sight of Jacko Chang.

The three of them fanned out, searching and calling for him, but it was hopeless. They discovered an open window opposite the closet that Leah had been locked in. "He must have climbed out as soon as my back was turned..." a stunned Leah claimed helplessly. "Oh, Tony, I was so focussed on you that I let him go."

Sparks' posture straightened with disappointment, but instead of giving Leah a criticism, she said, "It wasn't your job to stop him; it was mine."

That was when Firestone realised her criticising posture wasn't aimed at Leah; she was facing the bomber's workstation.

The bomber, and the bomber alone, had killed Sparks' entire team. He was here and Firestone felt paint drying on his fingertips from when he brushed the bomber's painted message. The bomber's message was fresh; they were that close and Sparks knew it.

Sparks wanted the bomber, Firestone wanted Scarleto, and Fong wanted Chang. This case was becoming dangerously personal.

Worse than that, Chang had only delivered on part of his promise to Sparks and Firestone; he gave them Leah, but there would be no statement from Chang regarding the rest of his and Scarleto's operations; that meant more work for them, but now that he knew Leah was safe, he was looking forward to it.

"Come on," he said as he supported a lady with each arm and guided them back to the surface. "We have work to do."

Chapter 5

Firestone and Sparks dropped Leah off at the FBI office. From there, she would be examined by doctors, cleaned up, and debriefed. She would also need to be evaluated to determine if she could return to active duty. Leah needed to be physically and mentally approved for general duty first and if she was able to return to work, whether she could work the Sapphire Theatre bombing without jeopardizing the integrity of the information she had already worked so hard to collect would have to be debated before Leah could join the taskforce.

As badly as he wanted to stay with Leah, Firestone knew that she would appreciate Scarleto's capture more than a few more awkward conversations with him, so he and Sparks dropped the vehicle they had borrowed from Chang off at the forensics garage, changed into more appropriately professional work attire, borrowed a new vehicle from the FBI motor pool, and drove to the damaged Sapphire Theatre.

The Sapphire Theatre was an extraordinarily opulent and architectural building both inside and out. The architect that designed it supposedly tried to model the outside after ocean waves, but it turned out looking more like a cut blue gemstone which was how it got the name the Sapphire. The architect also supposedly took inspiration for the inside of the theatre from some of the finest churches and classic opera houses; that architect pulled everything together well.

The interior of the Sapphire was an amazing mix of woods, metals, and rich fabrics. It blended rich purple curtains with deep reds in the velvet of the floors and seats. It also had white walls with soft cream and gold accents and the doors were solid and elaborately decorated wood.

Rails marking the aisles blended metals via a twisted pattern and they had a natural sparkle that tied them in with the rest of the room beautifully.

The mural on the ceiling and the odd tastefully-placed stained-glass window worked together to depict an image of angels enjoying a production of Cinderella on the theatre stage from the heavens, but the depiction was *almost* over shadowed by elaborate chandeliers that were also a part of the ceiling.

At least, that was what it used to look like; post-bombing, the heart of the theatre was a mashed navy-blue plume of smoke damage and broken lights. Sparks and Firestone efficiently weaved their way through the carnage and the mass of law enforcement responders until they found Dawson Sour.

Sour was a friend of Sparks' from her local crime lab and was apparently vital to law enforcement reaching a solution to the Carlton Tower horror, but Firestone didn't even know he was alive until Sparks and her boss Snowden gave him glowing recommendations for the taskforce.

From a distance, Sour looked like an eager college intern. He was roughly five-foot-seven, had crazy red hair that looked styled-by-electrical-socket, and well groomed auburn facial hair. He wore large silver glasses and a dark grey lab coat that sported the insignia of the lab he worked in.

According to Sparks, people underestimated Sour because of youth, his sense of enjoyment in his job, and his wild scientist's appearance, but Sparks insisted that Sour was a genius and Firestone was eager to see him prove that he belonged on the taskforce.

"Tell me what we're looking at Sour." Sparks said as they reached his side. They were standing over a charred corpse.

"So far, six people are dead; three people from this row of seats and three from the row behind them. The bomb was what I would call a burner not a vaporizer." Sparks and Firestone unimpressed by Sour's glee over information that wasn't helpful.

Sour straightened up and explained more clearly, "Bombs usually blow people apart or even vaporize them with the explosion, but as we can see by our friend here…" He pulled their attention to the corpse near them, "He's burned not separated into a dozen pieces; this suggests that the bomb that was used here was more of a flamethrower than it was an explosive device."

Everyone nodded understandingly and Sour continued, "It still did a good job though because..." as Sour spoke, he turned their attention to the roof above them. Sour used a flashlight to show that the ceiling was burned through to the point that they could see speckles of the sky above it. The burned patch fanned out from where they were standing out to the stage in a near perfect circle. The structural damage was bad, but it was worsened when Sour explained, "Twenty-three other people sustained severe burns and other injuries when pieces of the building's structure fell on them."

"These guys placed their device well considering their goal; any further back from the stage and the damage it did would have been greatly reduced..."

Firestone started pacing in an agitated fashion; he only stopped when a coroner came and collected the corpse. "What's up?" Sparks asked.

"This bomb is different from the devices that were used to destroy the Carlton Tower; what if these aren't the same guys?" Sparks and Firestone eyed Sour nervously.

"You need to see is this," Sour shone his flashlight at the wall opposite the torn seats. On the wall were words. They were tough to make out, like a message written in pencil on grey paper, but they definitely had impact.

The words were, **'RESPECT THE CONTROL WE HAVE**

BFAPA'

Brotherhood For A Pure America. They somehow managed to build a message into their latest explosive device. They were definitely back.

"Also, several witnesses describe an older gentlemen with walking difficulties in a brightly coloured, out of style suit talking to himself and examining his pocket watch, which was apparently the bomb... isn't that your man Scarleto?"

Scarleto did have crippling injuries and he had reputations for both mindless self-talk and an almost clown-like wardrobe, but just like at the Carlton Tower, something didn't seem right to Firestone.

Scarleto was more of a shot-caller than a suicide bomber and if this was, for some reason, Scarleto's swan song, why would he have left such an obvious gap in the revenge puzzle; Firestone's conclusion was that he wouldn't. Firestone felt he knew what he had to do next.

Firestone thanked Sour for his preliminary information than turned to leave the theatre. "Firestone, where are you going?" Sparks called after him.

"I have a hunch that if they are cocky enough to have their bomb write a message on the wall, they're cocky enough to raise hell with whomever else they met the first time around; including Rebecca Whales..."

Chapter 6

Rebecca Whales was the country's favorite reporter. She had a phenomenal record for keeping her stories truthful and informative, which kept the feminine audience tuned in, and she was also a super-attractive young blonde that had a body that every underwear model strived for, which grabbed the male audience.

The Brotherhood reached out to Whales after their first attack to spread their false message, but Firestone turned their outreach back on them. Firestone worked with Whales to set a trap for the terrorists in which Whales made a request during a broadcast for a face-to-face meeting with the terrorist leader that had called her. The terrorist, later identified as John Murphy Bell, reached out again, a meeting was arranged, and Firestone went along disguised as a cameraman.

Unfortunately, Whales reacted too boldly when Bell showed up to the meet and she sent Bell running, but because the physical exertion aggravated his sickened state, Bell got a nose bleed and his bleeding nose left a blood trail that was later used to identify him.

Firestone felt that was necessary to leave the theatre scene and go be Whales temporary bodyguard for several reasons. Firstly, Whales was the gap in Scarleto's revenge puzzle. It was very possible that the group could have credited the stunt with

Whales for their downfall and likely hated her. Firestone felt that, because they hated her so much, they might attempt retribution.

Secondly, if the group did go after Whales, the group would get tons of publicity.

Because of what happened the first time around, Whales had been dubbed television's foremost expert on the Brotherhood and was now on every channel every day because of her expertise.

Firestone's hunches had been right so far and he was certain he could not let the Brotherhood get a grip the public again, so he left the scene at the Sapphire in the competent hands it was in and dropped by the field news station where Whales was currently working.

Firestone strolled in to the BMN newsroom just as they were cutting to a commercial break. Whales was right at home at the anchor desk. The desk was a promotion that she earned from years of hard work and high ratings, but the spotlight that the Brotherhood had given her helped to put a rush on it.

She had cut her hair and dyed it about two shades of darker brown since she and Firestone had last met and she was wearing a slightly more appropriate black dress than her usual lingerie-type costuming, but she still looked better prepared for a hot date than she was to deliver a top story.

When the bell rang signaling that the cameras had stopped rolling, Whales got up and wrapped Firestone in a gentle hug just as if they were old friends. "I'm thrilled that you're here Tony," she said as they parted, "We can put you on the show after the break." Whales attempted to flag down a crewman who would set him up with microphones, but Firestone stopped her.

"I'm not here to be your expert guest," He explained. "I'm here to watch over you..."

Whales became laser-focussed on Firestone, "Am I being threatened?"

Firestone wasn't sure how to answer that question because they hadn't threatened Whales; at least, not yet. Firestone didn't want to lie that they did because he had good reason to worry that his lies could end up on the air and that would be a mess, but if he told the truth Whales would drop her guard. If she relaxed, she would be at greater risk and he would have no choice but to sit in her guest chair.

Given his lack of good options, he answered with an authoritative look. Whales' producer warned everyone in the room then that it was two minutes until camera role and that everyone should take their positions for broadcast.

Whales listened; she turned back towards the anchor desk and Firestone stepped back respectfully. He expected her to walk up and get settled into her seat, but she didn't. Rebecca Whales simply stood there; she was staring at something.

She spun around and asked the production crew, "What are those next to my coffee?"

Firestone looked past her and saw two black roses lying across the table next to Whales' black coffee mug. Firestone could see a note attached to the flowers and walked up to examine it. As he walked, he pulled on blue latex gloves. Whales' producer was disquieted by Firestone's interest and shifted the broadcast to an on-the-scene reporter, so Firestone could investigate without the public's eye tainting what he found.

Firestone turned the roses over and read the note. It said, 'ONE ROSE BECAUSE YOU'RE LOVED AND ANOTHER BECAUSE NO ONE'S GRAVE SHOULD BE EMPTY. YOUR LIES BLACKENED BOTH. TELL OUR STORY RIGHT THIS TIME AND YOU'LL ONLY NEED ONE.'

Firestone shot Whales a look that said 'you have your threat', but she wasn't looking at him. Whales had her back to Firestone and she was talking on her cell. She then turned suddenly and called for her producer's attention as she simultaneously ended her call. She demanded that they go live. The next time Whales looked at Firestone she took her seat and shoed him off of the set.

Firestone knew as soon as he had stepped away that the terrorists had more lies to tell. Firestone decided to stay and listen; what he would believe would have to be determined by his investigation.

Chapter 7

"Hello America," Rebecca said soberly as the cameras swooned over her, "We interrupt our developing story on the Sapphire Theatre Bombing to play you a message from the group that is claiming responsibility for it."

Firestone attempted to rush the set. Listening to how Whales interpreted what someone else had told her was one thing, but a direct message was completely different. If Whales was regurgitating someone else's words, the person who talked to her was technically a protected source, at least until the investigators could prove the information given tied the informant to terrorism or other ongoing severe crimes; a direct message, however, was legal evidence.

The FBI had the right to examine the tape before it aired. He also knew a live recording would send the city into panic, the administration of every law enforcement agency would be infuriated, the terrorists would be empowered, and the investigation would potentially be tainted; but the production security and flow crews all halted Firestone as Whales pressed play.

A deep but youthful voice with an unidentifiable accent said, "You called us dumb and you called us gutless, but we are neither;" Firestone remember those words from the bomber's message back at the

Laundromat and then listened with hypersensitivity.

"We are the Brotherhood For A Pure America and we promised more attacks if we did not see changes, but you chose to believe your leaders over us and do nothing, so we kept our word. We attacked the Sapphire Theatre because it featured an Italian opera instead of an American play. We don't need outside influences to have culture."

Firestone felt that was odd; a person with an exotic accent putting down migrant influences...

"We do not enjoy shedding blood because death empties families, but we are prepared to keep doing it for the greater good. Let's hope this is the last time you hear from me." The caller hung up and after about four minutes of tense reporting the station cut to a recap of the Carlton Tower disaster from months earlier because the terrorist had referred the previous event.

As the recap played, Firestone marched up to Whales and angrily explained, "You should have alerted me to that call. We could have run a trace on it, instead, you not only killed a potential opportunity to arrest another terrorist, but also his words made every law enforcement agent look incapable of protecting anyone."

She shook her head emotionally, but he kept on, "I am right here; if he was threatening you, you should have trusted me to protect you."

"Tony, he's here too." She inconspicuously glanced towards the door that Firestone had entered through. Firestone saw a young, sweaty, African male who was dressed in heavy clothes approaching the anchor desk. Firestone realized that he must of made Whales aware of being there during his call to her.

Firestone recognized the young man because Firestone and his team had formally identified him following the group's escape after the Carlton Tower disaster. He was Pierre Mambossa, Scarleto's bomb-maker.

Firestone knew that Mambossa's presence here was not a sign of good tidings. Firestone watched Mambossa's every move intently as he slowly braced for conflict by drawing his gun. Unfortunately, the production crew caught on to the intensity and tuned the cameras on Firestone and the unidentified male who said, "Now that we have your attention, it is important you remember us."

The unidentified man then pulled open his thick jacket to unveil a suicide bomb vest. He pulled a dead-man's switch from his jacket pocket and pressed the button. In the same nanosecond, Agent Firestone drew his gun and fired.

Time slowed for everyone in the newsroom as they watched a dead Pierre Mambossa fall to floor; blood leaked from a hole square in Mambossa's forehead. Mambossa had been cocky and designed detonator that would activate the vest if the button was released after being pushed and Firestone's shot killed all muscle function in Mambossa's body; still, Firestone got industrial tape from a crewman and taped Mambossa's thumb on the detonator and wrapped it several times to ensure it was secure.

Suddenly, Rebecca Whales screamed, "Tony, he's going to shoot you."

Firestone looked up to see three members of the original Golden Dragons in the newsroom doorway; one was poised to shoot and the others were watching proudly.

Firestone's hands were tied securing Mambossa's suicide vest. There was no way Firestone could defend himself and a brief chill piped through his veins as he accepted death.

Suddenly, a string of shots rang out. Firestone cringed and jumped back at the sound. He expected blood and pain, but he quickly realised he wasn't wounded and that the gangsters who had him pinned were now down on the ground.

Firestone drew his weapon and went out to investigate what had happened. He found that the three gangsters in the newsroom doorway were dead and as Firestone kicked their weapons a safe distance away, he found one of Chang's loyal enforcers that he'd met back at the restaurant about to die further down in the newsroom parking lot.

Firestone rushed over and knelt next to him. With his dying breaths, the enforcer explained, "That bomber betrayed Scarleto and Wu. Wu dispatched the last of his army to try and collect him. Scarleto killed Wu as soon as they left."

The enforcer swallowed uncomfortably then said, "When they realized that you stopped him first, they tried to settle for you instead. I stopped them, but they were faster than I credited them."

The man gripped Firestone's hand, "I am the last of Golden Dragons, old and new, outside of our king. Please forgive me for what I've done so that I may die beside a brother."

Firestone simply nodded and watched the light of life go out of the man's eyes.

Firestone realised that he confirmed that all of the Dragons were now dead except for Chang; Firestone wasn't exactly sure what to do with that information, so with the scene as secure as he could make it, Firestone made several phone calls. He called the bomb squad to secure the vest, he called Director Meyer to report the shootings and prepare for the press nightmare, and then he called Sparks.

As soon as he hung up, Firestone noticed Rebecca Whales standing between him and the closest camera. She said, "I would like to apologize to everyone that I may have frightened by playing that monster's call. I did as I was threatened to do, not what I believed in."

She gestured to Firestone in a game show host's fashion and said, "Thankfully, FBI Agent Anthony Firestone knew what they would do before they did it. He was here before I was even threatened because he was proactively brave."

She moved back so that she was standing beside him and finished, "I trusted him to save my life and not only did he save me multiple times, but he save all of us here in the BMN Newsroom. I'm confident he and the FBI will save us all; so if this false Brotherhood For A Pure America wants to threaten more attacks, I say, bring it on!"

Part Two – Lights, Camera, Nothing

Chapter 8

Special Agent Leah Fong was much improved from the ragged woman Firestone had rescued. It had only been about seven hours since Firestone had liberated her from her closet prison, but she called in a few favors and managed to get herself medically and psychologically checked, treated, and cleared in that time. She had also finished her debriefs with her handler and internal affairs and managed to squeeze in a hot shower, a heavy meal, and a decent night's rest.

Despite a few bad bruises on her hands and face and a line of stitches running from her right eyebrow down to her chin, she was back to her professionally high-styled and porcelain complexion-toting self.

She smiled softly to herself as she waited for Director Meyer to come in and speak with her. Director Meyer was going to inform her of his conclusion as far as whether she could join Firestone's taskforce or serve desk duty. In the meantime, the news was playing on a TV in the corner of the conference room she was waiting in.

The scene of Firestone shooting the would-be suicide bomber followed by Whales' emotional apology was playing on a continuous loop. The story made Fong smile for several reasons.

First, it showed the world the amazing man she always knew Firestone was. Second, she liked that it clearly caught him off guard and he looked adorable. Third, it left him standing with one of the city's most eligible bachelorettes and she felt that suited him perfectly. Still, she wished she was standing there with him instead of Whales.

Meyers marched in and turned a handshake into a hug. "You did a wonderful job Agent," Meyers said as they parted and took their seats.

"Thank-you sir, but the person who really deserves congratulations is Tony; he actually neutralized his suspects." She gestured to the television set.

Meyers laughed. "Agent Firestone has certainly been getting some positive publicity for himself and for the agency lately, but you are his equal. You went through hell and came back stronger." He showed her the results of her fitness tests. "You beat your original fitness and marksmanship scores from when you graduated from the War College. I have no concerns about your physicality."

Fong's gentle smile returned and Meyers continued, "Your mentality is more of a question however..." Leah's smile faded and she looked at Meyer with concern as she handed back her score sheets.

"You were tortured for months Leah; that is not something you can bounce back from by pretending it didn't happen…"

"I talked to the department shrink in detail about everything during my psychological evaluation…"

"I know," he said respectfully, "and the good doctor explained that she's satisfied that you're dealing with everything in a healthy way right now, but she's concerned that you may spiral if you investigate this case."

Leah listened with uncertainty as Meyers continued more slowly. "Clearly, the Sapphire Theatre Bombing is tied to Scarleto and, by Chang's own admission to Firestone, Scarleto is connected to Chang. If you investigate this case, we will no longer be able to charge Chang for assaulting you. Also, either Firestone or Liaison Detective Sparks will have to be the ones to formally arrest Chang. If you slap the cuffs on Chang, your statements regarding anything you saw or heard while working undercover will be invalid in court."

"If your undercover report is voided, we will still have some valid charges we can bring against Chang, but those charges will have him spending months in jail as opposed to years." Meyer then paused briefly to gauge Fong's ability to swallow his bittersweet words before making his true feelings clear.

"Having you work this case is risky as far as getting solid convictions are concerned, but also, I believe working this case is unfair to you. You deserve the justice *and the glory* that will come from this case, but under these circumstances, you will see very little, if anything, of either justice or glory. I also think that you've had more than your fair share of unfairness lately and I don't want it to compound inside you and break you down. You're a great agent and you deserve to have a long and glamorous career; I need agents like you to be here."

"I appreciate your words sir," she said after a moment, "But respectfully, I believe that distancing myself from this case would drive me crazier than simply not getting ideal results. I agree to the restrictions on me and I want in."

"Ok," Meyers said reluctantly. He slid her gun and badge across the table for her to take, then he added, "But you should also know that Rebecca Whales has put the world's eyes on you and your team. If you slip, it will end you in more ways than one, so I reserve the right to pull you out at any time."

"That's very fair," Leah said and, with a parting professional handshake, Special Agent Leah Fong made her way the BMN Newsroom to once again join her partner Agent Anthony Firestone.

When she arrived, Fong expected a warm reunion not unlike the one she experienced when Firestone first rescued her; but instead, she found herself walking into a wall of people.

Reporters from BMN and probably every other newsroom in the country were swarming Firestone and making it impossible for Agent Fong to get to him. After about a minute of awkward shuffling and elbowing, she gave up on trying to get to Firestone and settled for the small crime scene around the bomber's corpse, but although the bomber's body was far less popular than Firestone and Whales were, Agent Fong had to struggle through a thick crowd to get to it.

There was a relatively small eight-by-eight area taped off around the body which was now undressed and loosely wrapped in a body bag on a gurney. There was a uniformed officer guarding every edge of the crime scene tape and a pathologist was examining the body with her back to Fong; she looked like she was in her late teens and like she'd been pulled from an audition for 'Dream Girls.' There was also a forensic officer dividing her time between photographing and fielding forensics questions from the reporting hoard.

Fong was disappointed as she showed her badge to one of the uniformed officers and went under the crime scene line. She had hoped to have Firestone at her side and that they would be working with the other taskforce members that she'd heard so much about from Firestone during the ride from the Laundromat back to the FBI field office, but she had to settle for these strangers.

"I'm Special Agent Leah Fong," Leah said she knelt at the pathologist's side, "What are we looking at?"

The doctor looked her over briefly and disapprovingly before turning her attention back on the body, "Agent Firestone is a fantastic shot. Other than the bullet wound there are no obvious signs of trauma, so that is more than likely the cause of death. I had to wait for the Bomb Squad to remove the vest, but once the body was secured, I ran an electronic field fingerprint test which confirmed the ID that you guys put forward." The pathologist made some notes than zipped up the bag and carried the body out with help from one of the officers guarding the tape; she did so without giving Leah another look.

Leah shook off her discomfort and turned her attention to the other inattentive investigator. "I'm a new addition to this case," Leah explained cautiously, "Could you tell me, who was the bomber ID'd as?" The forensic photographer starred at Leah with a look that suggested that the photographer didn't believe Fong belonged beyond the tape. Needless to say, she didn't get an answer.

Leah was ready to give up on the BMN scene and go to the Sapphire Theatre in hopes of getting more direction when Donna Sparks ran in.

Fong watched Sparks artfully weave through the gang shooting crime scene to get in the door only to have an officer grab her before she made it under the tape, so she called to Fong, "Was it him? Did Firestone shoot Pierre Mambossa?"

Fong was lost. Based on what little she knew, Fong couldn't confirm if the body matched the name Sparks had just asked about and Fong did not yet understand why Sparks seemed so personally attached to this character and his death.

Fong could not hide her confusion as she meekly explained, "The pathologist that just left said Firestone's shooting victim's prints matched the ID that the FBI was expecting; whether that means it is Mambossa, I don't..."

Before Agent Fong finished, Sparks left. Leah Fong helplessly watched Sparks somehow do what she couldn't and successfully navigated the press-mob surrounding Firestone and Whales; Sparks then made it to the stage.

Sparks wondered up to Firestone and Whales with the grace and emotion of a zombie. She sandwiched herself between Whales and Firestone, grabbed Firestone's face, and pulled him into a passionate kiss. When they finally broke apart, Sparks thanked Firestone for killing the man who had killed her team.

The press-mob went off with a reignited fury. They asked if Firestone had considered the bomber's cruelty when he fired his key shot. They wanted to know who Sparks was, who her team was, and what her association to the bomber had been; but most of all, they wanted to suck up every second of the developing love triangle drama between Firestone, Sparks, and Whales as Whales was now sporting the appearance of a jilted and jealous lover.

With all the drama brewing on the stage, no one noticed Leah Fong's heartbreak as she helplessly watched her partner, best friend, and the man-of-her-dreams sharing a kiss with a woman she barely knew. No one her make a tearful and quick exit out of the back.

She fought back tears all of the back to headquarters, but once she got back to her desk, she had come to a realization. So much had changed in the months she was gone undercover and she couldn't adjust to the changes simply because she was so unprepared to work.

To remedy her situation, she worked late into the night familiarizing herself with her new case. She read every statement, every report, and every file; including the personnel files of every member of the taskforce that she'd be working with. She also combed over everything she could possibly read about Whales.

With her research completed, she created her own file which included everything that she felt was important about the personnel involved and detailed everything that every federal agency knew about both Scarleto and Chang.

With her file created for reference, she started developing her own leads to work. She carefully put out feelers that she hoped would lead to Chang and Scarleto's current whereabouts eventually.

She then contacted Angelique Marceau and lead pathologist Richard Kane.

Chapter 9

Firestone was excited as he walked in to work the next day. He had heard that Leah had been cleared for duty, been cleared for the taskforce, and had been working the crime scenes the previous evening. Firestone got so caught up with the shooting of the bomber, Whales, Sparks, the press flurry, and the post-action evaluation that followed the shootings that he couldn't have seen her even if he had been looking.

Now, however, the case had hit a bit of a stand-still; the bomber's death offered no new leads on where Chang or any other followers of the false terrorist group fueling the case were and he needed forensics to confirm if Scarleto was the Sapphire's suicide bomber. The stand-still did offer the much anticipated catch up time with his partner that Firestone had been looking forward to for months.

As he approached, he noticed that Leah was on the phone, so he paused so he didn't bother her. As he stood frozen, he briefly stared down at the trey of coffees and scones he bought on the way in. He smiled to himself as he reflected on the hundreds of times he had brought Leah a coffee like this; he was eager to see her smile, but before he made it into the bullpen, virtually every woman in the office swarmed him. They crowded him the same way teenage girls swarmed their favourite boy-bands, waving grocery store tabloids plastered with his picture.

They flirtatiously peppered him with questions about Donna Sparks and Rebecca Whales. They then pointed out what was on the TV; it was a glamour-pumped loop of the love triangle. Firestone was embarrassed to see that a ten-second-long romantic moment between him and Sparks was the showpiece that the whole world was glued to, but he was relieved that the impromptu reality show was overshadowing the fake terrorists and their terror fuel.

Unfortunately, Firestone was unable free himself from the love-fuelled swarm before Leah hung up her phone. They locked eyes briefly and she wrote a note that she left on her desk before she jogged downstairs; catch-up-coffee was off and Firestone was so eager to find out why that he cranked up his charm in a skillful effort to disband the barricading hoard.

He answered all of their questions truthfully and jovially. He denied any romantic feelings for both Sparks and Whales, citing that both women were emotionally charged by the bomber's death. He also gently reminded them about the terrorism and the lives lost and all of his coworkers returned to work with a bitter-sweet attitude.

Firestone left the breakfast trey on Leah's desk as he read her note. It called him down to the morgue.

When he got there, Fong wasn't there and Doctor Richard Kane was busily working with his back to Firestone. "Is that you T-

Bone?" Richard asked without turning around.

Richard Kane always looked more like an old-style New York butcher-slash- deli man than a medical examiner. His scrubs were always stained with evidence of his hard work and his hands were mangled from years of working in near-freezing conditions. Kane was also unshaven, grossly out of shape, had a greasy comb-over, and he had a strikingly sickly appeal; but all of the unappealing elements of Richard's appearance could be attributed his ridiculously demanding work schedule and love of cured meats and draft beer.

Despite his near-homeless and overworked image, Kane had managed to send tens of thousands of Carlton Tower victims home to their final resting places in a matter of weeks. He was a behind-the-scenes hero and once again, his morgue was filled with burned victims. Firestone stepped in next to one of those victims and spoke, "Yes, it's me Doc; where's Leah?"

Kane remained inattentive, "She asked me to confirm some details an informant had told her on the phone just now, so I updated her with the same information that I'm about to give you and then she got a call. After she hung up with whoever called her, she thanked me, and she called Angelique. I overheard her tell Angelique that an informant had come through on Chang's current whereabouts..."

"Great! I'll be right back," Firestone said as he headed for the door.

"Firestone," Doctor Kane said, finally turning. Firestone stopped cold with questions in his eyes. "Meet John Murphy Bell..." Kane answered as he gestured towards the body Firestone was standing next to. Firestone stared stunned; forgetting about Leah yet again.

Chapter 10

"How could this be Bell?" Firestone asked. His instincts told him that the man who has suicide bombed the Sapphire Theatre was not Scarleto, but admittedly, he was hoping he'd be wrong and that Scarleto would turn out to be dead; Bell's death was not only disappointing but confusing as well. "Bell was leading the charge..." Firestone said disappointedly.

"Not by a long shot," Kane interrupted, "The bullets you put in him months ago combined with an untreated Tower Toxin infection and some other wounds would have crippled him to the point of uselessness back then; I'm impressed he even made it to the theatre, which explains the struggle that the witnesses saw..."

Firestone nodded and inserted, "He probably dressed Bell like him so that witness statements would confuse us, but..." Firestone didn't know what else to say and that emptiness enraged him.

"So what the hell is this then? Was Chang correct when he told us that Scarleto was simply out for revenge? Is this Scarleto's revenge against Bell? What does Scarleto gain from trying to make Bell mirror him in death?" Firestone shouted in frustration.

"I don't know," Kane shouted back, "I'm sure not in that monster's head, but it sounded like Leah's informant sure was."

Firestone jogged out angrily and making it to Angelique's cubical made him even angrier. Normally, the sight of Angelique's plump Caribbean form spiced with modern hacker style made him smile, but he was angry that, like the morgue, Leah wasn't there and Angelique seemed busy.

"Please, tell me you have something for me," Firestone pleaded, but Angelique waved him off. Firestone rolled a chair around for himself, sat, and uncomfortably waited for her to finish.

"Merci," Angelique said as she stood and removed her headset. Thinking she was done, Firestone also stood and repeated his plea to be caught up on the goings on, but Angelique shut him down a second time.

She quickly made her way down the corridor with arms filled with new files, but she suddenly turned and said, "Actually, you should get Donna and stakeout the address on my screen there. Leah is meeting her informant there and it sounds like a big deal."

Part Three – A Shot In The Dark

Chapter 11

Firestone hated everything about this operation. First, his catch up time with Leah was cancelled. Next, he found himself staking-out an unfamiliar building while he waited for Leah, who he didn't see, to meet with an informant he didn't know in a building that would have made a tactical strike impossible. If things went south, they would all likely die.

Besides that, there was more immediate tension between him and Sparks. They had not had an opportunity to clear the air after the passionate kiss they had shared at the newsroom. Firestone decided to cut the tension by starting a neutral conversation, "Something that I've always wanted to know about you Donna is that you seem Israeli, but a name like Donna Sparks is as American as apple pie; why is that?"

Sparks chuckled, "My mother was Israeli, but my father was only half-Israeli. Our American last name came from my father's American father. I was born in my American grandparent's home and my parents left me with them in the hopes of giving me a better life..."

"It was my grandmother's decision to give me an American first name. She hoped it would help me fit in..."

She looked at him intently, "How about you Anthony? Firestone isn't exactly Italian..."

It was his turn to chuckle, "It's a similar story to yours actually; my mother was Italian, but my father was Native American actually made up our last name before they married."

"You're joking," Sparks interjected.

"No," Firestone asserted humorously, "My father was adopted, so our original last name would have been 'Wilson,' but my father had two problems with that name. He didn't believe that 'Wilson' was a cool enough surname and felt it didn't do justice to his heritage, so when he turned eighteen he legally changed his name to Firestone. He explained that he thought that fire was cool and that nothing in the world was more solid and reliable than a stone. He also believed

'Firestone' sounded more true to who he was ancestrally."

"He agreed to name me Anthony because he liked all of the cool nicknames he could get from it: Tony, Ant-man, T-Bone, and so on."

Sparks laughed with him for a minute, "Ant-man? Did anyone really use that one?"

"He did, all of the time, just to prove that someone could..." He said with a laugh.

Then the awkwardness returned. "I wanted to apologize for kissing you back at the newsroom..." she said finally.

Firestone waved her off casually, "I understood where you were coming from emotionally; I mean I am a ruggedly handsome super agent." He joked.

She giggled, but clarified seriously, "I have to admit, I did notice your awesomeness; mostly because you remind me of Raymond. Raymond was a member of my team that was killed by the bomber. I was also in love with him…"

Firestone listened intently and watched the tears well up in her eyes as she turned her gaze towards the windshield, "Raymond was smart and funny *and* he was a gifted investigator, but he also had a special way of making me feel like the most important person in the room. You remind me of Raymond because you are also good at all of those things, Firestone. I have to admit, I did have a little crush on you."

"Thank-you," he said softly, not wanting to interrupt.

She nodded, acknowledging his acceptance, and continued. "It was meaningless hero worship though; like you said, I was overwhelmed with gratefulness for the bomber being gone."

"The bomber took so much from me; I lost the man I loved, I lost my brothers in arms, and I was injured. I was overwhelmed with so many emotions when I learned the bomber was dead that words could not express how I felt towards you, so I sprang for actions, but that was wrong because I saw you and Leah together when you first rescued her. Chang was truthful, wasn't he? You and Leah are in love?"

"We never crossed any lines," Firestone answered carefully, "But Leah and I do have something deeper than our partnership. Or at least, we did have something; the atmosphere between us seems different since she went undercover..."

"That's not saying you're not wonderful though..."

"Thank-you Firestone, but I still feel foolish..."

"Don't worry about it; if anyone is making a mistake here, it's me for passing up on you..."

Sparks laughed again, "Well it's a mistake I'm glad you're making, we're not right for each other, but speaking of other woman you think are wonderful, where does Rebecca Whales fit into the equation?"

"Rebecca is a stunning woman, but she is too manipulative and drawn to the spotlight for my personal taste. I also think that if she took a serious look at what she really wanted, she would grab herself a handsome Hollywood man. I told her as much once things calmed down back at the newsroom; I phrased it more gentlemanly though."

"I think we both know where your heart lies and I'm confident that I will find where mine lies again." There was another tense moment between them before she finished with, "I think you should tell Leah how you feel. You shouldn't waste your time with Leah the way I wasted my time with Raymond."

"I will," He said seriously, but he was now focussed on the stakeout, "as soon as whatever this is is over."

Chapter 12

Firestone and Sparks sat for about a half an hour more before they finally saw Leah come out. She was talking on her cell and working the key fob to unlock the grey sedan that was parked ahead of them. She stopped before she reached the car though.

She looked around for a moment before seeing them. She waved and approached them. Leah hung up her phone while Sparks rolled her window down to hear what she had to say.

"My informant came through," Leah explained, "She said that the Sapphire Theatre bombing was another murder-for-hire. She said that Scarleto was hired to kill Gerry and Stella Devoroe."

The Devoroe's were two of the six people killed in the bombing; they were the two seated beside Bell and, interestingly enough, they founded the Asian Quarter and financed the build of the Sapphire Theatre.

"According to my informant," Leah continued, "The late Devoroe's son, Michael Devoroe, has a thing for cocaine and prostitutes. Apparently, Michael found out his parents planned to disinherit him and he intended to kill them before they could cut him off, but my informant told me that Scarleto initially refused the Devoroe job; he only accepted after he and Chang had a fight."

Firestone remembered what Chang had told him the night of the bombing.

Scarleto had plans drawn up to blow up Firestone's FBI Field Office, which was probably why Scarleto initially refused Michael Devoroe's offer. Then, Chang boldly refused to be Scarleto's pawn, leaving Scarleto desperate for dramatic revenge against Chang and Chang's mother was at the theatre when it was bombed. She was unharmed, but the message was clear to Chang.

With everything that had happened following the Carlton Tower's collapse and Chang's new hatred, Scarleto was rapidly losing money and connections. Michael Devoroe was offering to pay. If Scarleto got a cash infusion, Firestone believed the threat to his office would be back on and Scarleto would be virtually impossible to capture.

Luckily, Leah had more to offer, "My informant says that Michael Devoroe arranged a drop point to pay Scarleto. She believes that Chang knows where the drop point is and that he intends to kill Scarleto when he comes to collect his money."

"My informant doesn't know where the drop point is, but she does know where Devoroe is staying. I'm thinking we can find the drop point through Devoroe and be there to catch both Scarleto and Chang when the time is right."

They agreed and subsequently raided the motel where Devoroe was and with some assistance from SWAT, they arrested Devoroe and brought him into Sparks' precinct's interrogation room.

Chapter 13

In the interrogation room, Firestone and Sparks were standing behind Leah who was seated across from Devoroe. All of them were professionally dressed, emotionless, and menacing; they were stark contrast to their interviewee.

Devoroe's brown hair stood on-end in messy peeks. His eyes were sunken, bloodshot, and cupped by huge purple bags. His complexion was marred by heat rashes, dry-patches, and the desperate need of a shave. He was wearing a business-like blue button-up shirt and black kakis, but his clothes were so ruffled that they were barely on him and they were stained with dirt and puke. "You pigs have nothing on me," he mumbled.

"Oh no?" Leah asked knowingly as she slowly flipped out the crime scene photos of the Sapphire Theatre devastation. As she created her display in front of her victim, she spoke, "We have the man who did this in custody and he's already sniffing around for a deal."

They technically had the bomb-maker and the bomb deliverer in custody because Pierre Mambossa and John Murphy Bell were both dead and in the morgue. Obviously, neither of them were looking for a deal, but Firestone, Sparks, and Fong did not feel bad about stretching the truth with Devoroe.

He was a loser who sucked back drugs, devalued women, and killed his parents and four other people so he could avoid working and still support his habits with their money.

Firestone, Sparks, and Fong could have cared less about Devoroe's feelings and fate, but if they could convince him to give a full confession here, it would actually save Devoroe in the end and his lawyer wouldn't care about their fibs. The prosecution wouldn't care either because, ultimately, their actions were in the name of the greater good; they were being fair towards Devoroe and his confession could cause them to catch two of FBI's most-wanted.

Devoroe turned paler and Leah turned up the pressure, "Based on what he's told us so far, this was all your idea. If you don't make a counter-statement, you'll be facing several counts of murder with special circumstances."

"She means you'll be facing terrorism charges," Sparks chimed in.

"Terrorism charges carry a minimum sentence of ten years; maximums include life sentences at black-site prisons or death," Firestone added.

"Give me a pen and some paper..." Devoroe sputtered. "What's left of my family's fortune after these guys take their cuts isn't worth this terrorism shit."

Donna Sparks dropped a yellow pad of paper and some pens in front of Devoroe, but just as he started writing, Leah Fong strategically stopped him. She explained, "For this confession to be worth anything, we need details. We need names, dates, times if possible, and places. We need to know how you first got in touch with these guys right down to how you planned to pay them."

Devoroe's information paid off, but just barely.

By the time Devoroe finished writing his confession and they officially booked him into custody, it appeared that they would be too late to the money drop because the confession admitted that Devoroe had dropped the money off in the community lockers that were located at the base of the most popular running trail in Farber Memorial Park across town.

At this point, it was simply a matter of Scarleto going to collect the money and they thought it was possible that he had already come to collect his payment because the criminals had such a grand head-start. If that was the case, Scarleto could have already met his end at Chang's hand and then Chang would have disappeared.

When the three of them finally made into Farber Park, they stopped dramatically and parked illegally on the lawn in front of the lockers. They then ran over and Firestone cut the lock of Devoroe's locker with bolt cutters. Fong pulled the locker open and they all breathed a sigh of relief as she pulled three large gym bags from the locker and set them on the ground. They each unzipped a bag and saw bricks upon bricks of cash inside each.

    Suddenly, a gunshot rang out and Special Agent Leah Fong tumbled into Detective Donna Sparks.

Chapter 14

Firestone didn't think; he simply reacted the way he had been trained to. With his weapon drawn, he crouched so that the shooter would have to realign in order to get him and, in his new position, he surveyed the surrounding area for any signs of the shooter, but it was now after sunset. In the darkness and with the headlights of their suburban casting more shadows, he saw nothing.

As the seconds passed, his mind shifted from reacting to being concerned for Leah and Donna. He kept his gun as ready to use as he could while still staying low and crawling towards the women tactically. Once he made it to them, he used his phone as a flashlight so he could evaluate them in the darkness and what he saw was terrifying.

Leah was awake, but she was suffering severely. Firestone surmised that she must have been shot through the back because blood was bubbling from a wound on her chest, but the lockers were in front of her so the only solution was that the bullet came from behind and the bubbling was from the exit wound.

Judging by her current struggle and the way she fell into Sparks, Firestone also gathered that the entrance wound had hit more to Leah's side; meaning the bullet likely pierced a lung on its way out through her chest.

Donna Sparks was unconscious and trapped beneath Leah. Her face was bloodied, bruised, and swelling. It was clear to Firestone that Leah's head had clubbed Sparks when she fell and the clubbing broke Donna's nose and knocked her out.

Firestone was figuring out how he could move Leah off of Donna in order to allow her to breathe without worsening Leah's condition when another shot rang out. Once again Firestone reacted, but as he hoisted his weapon and searched for the attacker, he realised he couldn't breathe.

His mouth filed with blood and he began to choke on it. His consciousness waned and his strength fell out from under him. Like Leah, he had been shot through the back and the bullet likely pierced a lung on its way out through his chest. Also, by horrible coincidence, the bullet that had struck him went into Leah's stomach after it had passed through him. Firestone crumpled next to Leah as the pain sunk in.

"That's unfortunate," Scarleto's familiar scratchy voice said. Firestone could barely distinguish Scarleto's silhouette as he passed beside the headlights on his way to the money. "I had hoped to make Leah's shoulder match her other one; I guess my aim isn't as good as it was ten years ago."

Scarleto's casual approach gave Firestone enough time to gather himself, align, and shoot an unsuspecting Scarleto. At virtually the same moment that Firestone shot, two more shots came from Scarleto's previous position in the shadows beyond the headlights. The new shooter was Chang.

Because Chang had shot him twice and Scarleto was weighed down with the money bags; Scarleto fell on his face, but Chang was determined to see Scarleto's end and make it painful. He rolled Scarleto over to ensure Scarleto saw him repossess all of the money and poise his weapon for a fatal shot to his forehead.

Before Chang pulled the trigger, he explained, "You tried to kill my mother to show me that you have all of the power, but now I have the power. I am going to take your money and your life. Once you're dead, I will use your money to destroy everything that you've left behind."

Chang clearly didn't believe anyone else was alive and he wasn't exactly wrong. Firestone was passed the point of being able to shoot, Leah was worse than he was, but then Sparks shot Chang dead.

Sparks' injuries were far less severe than the rest of the group's were. She recovered enough to remove Leah's gun from its holster because her own gun was trapped underneath her. Sparks then used Leah's gun to neutralize Chang.

As all five of them laid there, clinging to survival by frayed threads, they heard the sirens of backup arriving from a grave distance.

"Since it's likely we're all going to die here today," Firestone said. His mouth filled with blood and his chest burned with every word, but he had to know. "Scarleto, what did you do with the girls?"

"I plan to survive this you know. I plan to survive and escape, but since I have always enjoyed playing games with you and your lovely partner, I will give you a clue. You were right the first time."

Firestone would have laughed out loud if his wounds would have allowed it because Scarleto's words had confirmed that his hunch about the bunker was always right. "Are they dead?" Firestone pushed.

"Do you really think I would waste that much equity? I left them in my partner's care." Those were Scarleto's last words; his volume actually faded as he died.

Fortunately, Firestone knew that the partner Scarleto was referring to was a man named Victor Sopa. Sopa was a fierce Columbian warlord, but despite his violent outward reputation, Sopa was a businessman first and a murderer second. Firestone hoped Sopa's economic nature meant the girls were still alive.

"Donna," Firestone huffed, "In case no one else makes it back to the office, I trust you to tell Angelique that Victor Sopa has Scarleto's girls and that I was right about Africa."

"I will, I promise Tony, but I think you better speak with Leah..." Firestone could see that Sparks had wrapped herself around Fong so that her hands were applying pressure to Leah's wounds, but Leah's blood was still soaking Donna's fingers. Leah's breathing had become a much greater struggle since she had first been shot and her pupils were dilating. Her injuries were so severe that she was likely next to die.

Firestone used all of the strength he had left to crawl over to Leah. As he settled in, closer to her, he squeezed her hand.

"T-tony," Leah spoke in a shrill whisper.

"I'm here Leah and I need you to stay with me because I'm in love with you."

He was glad he spoke quickly because he lost his ability to speak as soon as he'd finished.

"I'm glad to hear you say that because," she paused to wheeze a while. Firestone squeezed her hand tighter to encourage her to stay with him; it worked, but when she started speaking again her voice was quieter and higher. "I realized that going undercover was a mistake because I was in love you too."

"I wanted every person I saw and every voice on the phone I heard to be yours. I've really missed you, but you'll be alright…" Leah's voice faded out and her wheezy breathing stopped.

Firestone tried to move to wake her, but he had no strength and no air left in his chest. He was forced to keep lying still and let everything go black.

Chapter 15

The next thirty hours past agonizingly slowly for Angelique Marceau; for the first time in her career as an FBI Analyst, Angelique had no sense of what to expect.

She drove dangerously to this hospital that she could no longer remember the name of and robotically plopped herself in this waiting area. Her husband settled in beside her. For a while, they prayed together for positive news to come from the doctors responsible for Firestone, Fong, and Sparks then she ran over the frightening events that led her here with him.

"You remember the night that Leah called me late?" He nodded and she explained, "That was just after her undercover mission ended."

"Leah was upset about Firestone being caught in the famous love triangle because she herself had romantic feelings for him. Those two have been dancing around their feelings for each other for years, but in classic Fong and Firestone frustrating fashion, she did not want to put Firestone on the spot by telling him how she felt. After everything else Leah had been through, she wasn't sure whether she could handle the stresses and sacrifices that came with such a complicated relationship."

"Leah always preferred to struggle through her feelings in silence while burying herself in her work, but she was struggling to make the adjustment from the gang underworld to the anti-Scarleto taskforce; she needed a friend to help her organize her thoughts and I was that friend."

Angelique husband nodded understandingly and Angelique continued.

"That night, I filled Leah in on every juicy detail of Firestone's personal and professional accomplishments. I believe she found my information both helpful and settling. I believe that I helped her realise that Firestone hadn't changed as much as she'd first thought."

"The next day, Leah seemed back to her old self as an investigator. She was no longer side-tract by the romantic affairs that the case was stirring and she had found her own leads; one of those leads paid off."

"I didn't know the identity of the informant that had come through for Leah, but I assumed, because the informant knew both Scarleto and Chang, that she was someone Leah had encountered undercover."

"The next thing I really remember is hearing them all breathing relieved sighs over my headset because they were able to confirm the payoff hadn't been made yet."

"I expected to hear them think up a strategy for how they were going to capture both criminals..." She paused as she became a lot more emotional, "Then I heard a gunshot and the sound of them suffering and crumpling in chaos instead of making arrests."

"I started screaming: 'Shots fired on federal officers that are operating in Farber Park by the blue public lockers. Get out there, now!' into my headset."

"Once backup was called, I had no choice but to listen as words and more gunfire were exchanged. I heard Amilio Scarleto and Jacko Chang, so I knew that things were bad and the reports from the supporting officers only made it worse because they asked for assistance from a coroner."

"Had Leah's informant truly come through for her, or did the mystery informant set Leah and the team up for a fall?" Her husband could see Angelique blamed herself for not doing more legwork to identify the informant and verify the information she gave.

He knew that Angelique worried for every field agent that she worked with, but every time Firestone and Fong went out it was she felt that they were indestructible; they always came home and Angelique had come to rely on their constancy. Their deaths would change her forever and he wondered whether she would survive if they didn't make it home this time?

Suddenly, Firestone appeared, standing tall like an angel in the hall behind her. He was wearing a plain white T-Shirt and black jeans with the retail tags of the hospital gift shop still attached to them.

His hair was messy, his eyes were bloodshot and glazed with pain medication, his skin was ghostly pale, and he had blood dripping down his arms from where he'd likely torn out his IV's; but, as rough as he looked, he seemed over-the-moon happy about *something.*

"Angie," he said, "Leah and I are both alive and we're getting married..."

Angelique was so overwhelmed by the rollercoaster of emotions she'd been on that she fainted.

Part Four – Two Years Later

Chapter 16

Firestone adjusted his high-end suit jacket and straightened his matching black bowtie in the full-length mirror on the wall of his hotel room. This was the happiest day of his life and, fittingly enough, he looked the most handsome that he ever had.

Eighteen months of hospital treatments and physical therapy seemed to fly by for Firestone and Fong who were eagerly planning this day during their downtime at the hospital. It was their wedding day, and for the first time in what felt like forever, Firestone and Fong were genuinely thrilled.

As Firestone artfully tucked the red handkerchief with its sparkly silver veining into his outer breast pocket, he reflected on how far he and Leah come in such a short time.

From the moment he and Leah had met, Amilio Scarleto had been a dark cloud hanging over both their heads. The prospect of Scarleto's capture was an endless dream that kept them enslaved at the FBI.

It was a well-kept secret that Leah dreamt of becoming a lawyer and partnering with her brother, but Leah wanted to be there when Scarleto was taken down; or, at least, that was what she told him, but Firestone always wondered if Leah sensed the obsession inside him and stayed by his side in order to save him from himself. *Leah was his saviour; he looked forward to spending the rest of his life working to deserve her.*

Now Scarleto was dead and the missing women that Scarleto had taken hostage and turned into Firestone's personal ghosts had since been freed from Scarleto's long-time partner Victor Sopa.

Firestone was admittedly jealous about not being there to see the Scarlet Orchid wilt and the women freed, but he wouldn't have traded anything that brought him here.

Despite the fact that they weren't there personally, it was Firestone's information that led to Sopa's arrest and with Sopa's arrest, Scarleto's organization fell.

Because they were members of the original taskforce and had solved the mission once and for all thanks to Scarleto's dying confession, Agents Firestone and Fong became the two most famous federal agents alive. Their actions had virtually created world peace.

In the shooting that took down Scarleto though, Firestone and Fong were both injured and their injuries were severe enough to force them into retirement from the FBI.

Leah took the opportunity to become a lawyer and start working with her brother as she always dreamed and Firestone became a contracted private investigator for their firm.

Their new careers let them stay partners and paid twenty times better.

Firestone was exactly where he wanted to be; his enemies were vanquished, his career at the FBI ended in a glamorous blaze of glory, he had a satisfying new job, and he was marrying the woman he loved most in the world.

His groomsmen; which included his younger brother, Angelique's husband, Dawson Sour, and Richard Kane, crowded him out at the mirror. *It was time for the ceremony to start.* The group of gentlemen scuttled down to the first floor ballroom. It was a golden fairytale room embellished with red roses and purple rose petals.

Before he knew it, Firestone's groomsmen were linking arms with Leah's bridesmaids: Angelique, Leah's brother's girlfriend, Donna Sparks, and Rebecca Whales. They were all dressed in flattering red dresses and carrying bouquets of red roses.

The linking of their arms was carefully choreographed to the romantic piano blasting from strong speakers and Firestone followed the bridesmaids and groomsmen to the same music.

He smiled to all of their friends and family in eager attendance, but he felt his nerves begin to kick in as he reached the end of the isle.

The music slowed and softened as Leah's four year old niece stumbled down the aisle spilling rose petals from a white basket that matched her white dress. She gave everyone, including Firestone, a chuckle as she pounced on her mom upon getting to the end of aisle. Leah's brother's girlfriend fluidly handed her off to her mother and then everyone watched with amazement as Leah entered.

The crowd stood breathlessly and Firestone laughed with joy at what he saw. Leah's proud brother was arm in arm with her in a handsome black suit. He wore a red tie which highlighted the roses in Leah's extravagant bouquet and her bright red lipstick on her radiant smile.

Leah's hair was done up in a looser style with crystals spread throughout it which coordinated with the sparkling veil she was wearing. Her dress was white lace with delicate lace straps. It was a slender fit and Firestone later learned it was from the Stella York Spring collection from 2016 and she loved it from the moment she saw it in the store.

Leah's brother kissed Leah on the cheek and shook Firestone's hand before taking his front-row seat and the ceremony started with the standard welcoming and loving blessings.

Firestone was in a lovesick daze until the preacher asked for his vows. He said, "Leah, you've amazed me from the first moment that we met. You are beautiful and brilliant *and* you could easily beat me in a fight." The crowd chuckled, tears welled in Leah's eyes, and Firestone continued passionately.

"As I got to know you better and better over the years, I fell more deeply in love with you because I saw a light in you that shines brighter than book smarts or resourcefulness."

"Despite everything you've been through, you've come out kind. You've learned from every experience and you've shared those lessons with me, making me a better man."

"I miss your light when you're gone and I miss your kindness even more. I look forward to never having to spend another day wondering where you are and where your light is. How did I get so lucky?"

"Thank-you," the preacher said as the emotional crowd settled. "Leah," he gestured softly, "whenever you're ready..." It was her turn to say her vows, but before she couldn't because she needed a minute to collect herself. Leah's brother popped up and handed Leah a wad of tissues.

After a moment of Leah laughing through her tears, she unfolded the papers she'd written her vows on and kept tucked in her bouquet. She looked at her audience and jovially said, "He promised that he wouldn't make me cry and he lied, not the best way to start off a marriage."

The crowd and Firestone chuckled. Once they quieted, she looked up from her papers and into Firestone's eyes as she said, "I wrote down about a dozen things that amaze me about you too."

She gestured to her papers and said, "This says something about how much I love how you never give up, how much you make me laugh, and how deeply I love you because you always make it obvious how much you love me."

"This sounded perfect when I wrote it and I stand by every word, but now the only thing that sounds right is to tell you that I am the lucky one..."

A few more quick words were said and then Firestone and Fong sealed their vows with a passionate kiss. They then ran through a rain shower of rice and rose petals and smiled for photos.

They then danced the night away at their reception.

He twirled her around to the beat of the same Celtic music from the same Celtic band they had danced to the night before she left for the undercover mission that had started them on this journey. He remembered thinking that she was the most beautiful woman in the world back then; that night, he was left feeling angry at himself for not telling her how he felt.

Now, she was even more beautiful and this time, she wasn't leaving ever.

They would live happily ever after and they would leave nothing unsaid ever again.

Made in the USA
Middletown, DE
04 May 2017